Anne Fine

Gnomes, Gnomes, Gnomes

with illustrations by
Vicki Gausden

Barrington Stoke

For Angus

First published in 2013 in Great Britain by
Barrington Stoke Ltd
18 Walker Street, Edinburgh, EH3 7LP

www.barringtonstoke.co.uk

ISBN: 978-1-78112-204-4

Printed in China by Leo

Contents

Chapter 1
Oh, Sam! Please! Not *Again*!

I blame Mrs Pratt.

Mrs Pratt's our art teacher. We do art once a week. Sometimes we get out the paints and slosh them about a bit. Sometimes we make things out of stuff like glue and paper and the insides of loo rolls, like babies do. (Mrs Pratt liked the flying pig I made. And the crocodile, even if she did think it was a lady in a boat.)

But sometimes we get to use clay.

I love clay. I love to rip great lumps of it out of the big clay bin. I love to bash it. (I pretend it's that bully Chopper's face.) I love slapping water on it to make it softer. (Chopper's face again.) I love sticking my fingers deep into it to make holes.

I even love the funny way it smells.

Most times when we do clay in art class, I make gnomes. You know – the sort you see in gift shops and garden centres. I make all sorts – happy gnomes, grumpy gnomes, sad gnomes. Old gnomes with fishing rods in their hands. Young gnomes about to toss a ball into the air. Baby gnomes crying.

Then Mrs Pratt comes round. "Oh, Sam! Please! Not *again!*" she says. "Not *more* gnomes. Can't you try something else? Just for once. Just for me. *Please?*"

But I love making gnomes. I love rolling the clay to make the toadstool stem so fat and sturdy that it won't fall over. I love patting down the toadstool top till it's as smooth as a bald man's head.

Then I make the gnome himself. I start with short sausages that I'll shape into legs later. I make the solid little body, and poke the end of my pencil into the clay to make a row of buttons down his jacket. I roll the top lump of clay into a sort of head shape. I borrow my mate Arif's comb to carve in strands of hair.

Then I make the pointy hat to plonk on top. I shape it like an ice cream cone, then turn it over and shove it down hard on the gnome's head. I spend the rest of the lesson getting the arms and legs right. (Gnome fingers aren't too hard, but gnome boots can be tricky.)

And then the buzzer goes for the end of class. I take the gnome up to Mrs Pratt so she can put it on the shelf of stuff she's going to put in the kiln. That's a huge oven for baking clay.

"Oh, not another gnome!" Mrs Pratt says again. "How long have you been in this school, Sam? Because I must have put *hundreds* of these things into the kiln for you. What do you *do* with them when you take them home?"

Chapter 2
Then Mum Starts In On Me

Well, the first thing I do when I get home is get my gnomes painted. I don't do it myself. (I'm rubbish with a paintbrush. My hands just won't stay steady.) So I hand over all my gnomes to my sister Alice.

Alice gets out her paints and makes a great job of them. She spends hours on each one, letting one colour dry before she starts on another. So they have spotted hats, and stripy trousers, and jackets with silver stars.

Sometimes she does them in football colours.
(Liverpool and Norwich, mostly, because red
and yellow are her favourite paints.) Sometimes
she does them in wimpy pastel colours,
especially the baby gnomes. That takes ages
because she has to rinse her brush a hundred
times as she goes along.

She leaves them on the telly till they're dry, and then she gets out the varnish and brushes it all over. Now they glisten and gleam. They look *terrific*.

Then Mum starts in on me. "No, Sam! Not another gnome! I cannot stand to see them staring at me all the time I watch the telly."

"They're not staring at you," I tell her. "They're just sitting there, minding their own business. They're not doing any harm."

But Mum gets ratty. "No, Sam! I've told you a hundred times. You may not fill this house up with your gnomes. If you must keep them, take them up to your bedroom. Or out to the garden shed."

But I can't have the gnomes in my bedroom. I can't explain it, but they give me the creeps. I shut my eyes. And I feel sleepy. But then I get the weird feeling that some of them are watching me.

Really watching me, I mean. With proper eyes that work and brains behind them, deep inside the clay. I have to keep opening my eyes to make sure that they look exactly the same way they did when I got into bed.

Just plain old gnomes made out of clay.

So what I do is put them in the shed. When Dad was with us, he kept all his tools and paints in there. But now the shelves are crowded with my gnomes. I must have *hundreds*. Last year I counted, and there were 68.

And I've made lots since then.

Chapter 3
Disaster!

One morning, Mum's phone rang. It was Mrs Fry next door. Mum chatted with her for a while, and then rang her friend Nancy.

And then – disaster! Mum turned to Alice and me and said that Mrs Fry wanted to get rid of all the old stuff in her loft. "If I take it away, Mrs Fry says that Nancy and I can sell it in a car boot sale, and keep the money," she said. "So I'm going to put the whole lot in the shed till Nancy can come round tomorrow with her van."

"There's not much room in the shed," Alice warned her.

"There must be," Mum said. "I haven't put a thing in there since your dad left."

"But Sam has," said Alice.

Mum turned to me. "So what's in there, Sam?"

"Gnomes," I admitted.

"*Gnomes?*" Mum rolled her eyes, and went outside. I followed her. She unhooked the door to the shed and looked inside. She stared, then threw up her hands. She was so cross. "Sam! I had no idea! You've used up every shelf! The place is stuffed with gnomes! Where am I going to store all Mrs Fry's stuff till Nancy gets here tomorrow?"

"You could leave it out on the grass," I said.

"No, I can't," Mum said. "If it rains in the night, most of the things will be *ruined*."

"I don't see why."

"Because they will get *wet*."

"So?"

"Sam, not everything in the world is waterproof. Take it from me, I need the shed. Your gnomes will have to spend the night in your bedroom."

All of them? In my bedroom? All night? Over a hundred of them, watching me while I was trying to sleep?

No fear.

"No fear!" I told Mum.

But she was all fired up. "Well, they'll have to go somewhere else and I'm afraid I don't care where. That is your problem, Sam. All that I'm telling you is that I want every last gnome out of this shed by 5pm tonight."

"5pm?" I said. "That doesn't give me enough time to find a home for them."

But Mum had turned away. "I'm sorry, Sam. I'm just too busy to listen. I have to help Mrs Fry clear out her loft. She has workmen coming first thing tomorrow so she wants it done *right now*."

And off she went.

Chapter 4
They Have to Go *Somewhere*!

Alice was sitting on the back step, reading a comic.

"Alice," I said, "will you please let me put all my gnomes in your bedroom? Just till Mum and Nancy have sold the stuff from Mrs Fry's loft, and I can put them back in the shed?"

"No fear!" said Alice. (She's picked up that phrase from me.)

"Why not?"

"Because they'd scare Grey Rabbit. And Leo. And Topper. And Bunny Bear. And Little Green Dragon. And – "

I broke in fast, to stop her going on with the list of all the seven billion trillion frillion soft toys that she keeps in her bedroom.

"Oh, please!" I begged. "They have to go *somewhere*."

She waved a hand. "Why don't you leave them on the lawn till the shed's empty again?"

"They might get stolen," I told her.

Alice just laughed.

"All right," I admitted. "Maybe you're right, and nobody else would want them. But if it rains, they'll get wet."

Alice glanced up at the sky. "It doesn't *look* as if it's going to rain."

I was still worried. "Maybe not. But what if it *does*?"

Alice shrugged. "They should still be all right. They're varnished, so that means they should be waterproof."

"Really?"

"That's what it says on the tin."

"Show me."

She went inside to find the tin of varnish.
While she was gone, I read a page of her comic.
When she came out again, she pushed the
varnish tin in front of my nose and pointed to
a bit of tiny print on the back. It wasn't easy to
read, but I did see the word 'waterproof'.

That cheered me up a lot.

Chapter 5
You're Totally Bats

I set to and started on the job of taking all my gnomes out of the shed. I carried out armful after armful and dumped them on the lawn.

But I was still worried. I went to speak to Alice. "Do you think I should put them in black plastic bin liner bags?" I asked. "Just to protect them overnight?"

Alice thought that was a smart idea, so she ran off to the kitchen to fetch some. When she

came back, she said, "There are only three bin liner bags left. And Mum won't be happy if you use up the last of them."

"How many do you think I'd be allowed to have?"

Alice shrugged. "Two at the most?"

"Just *two*?"

Alice looked round at all the gnomes on the lawn. "It would be a squash if we stuffed them all into only two bags."

I tried to tell myself it wouldn't matter. "They're not going to *suffocate*," I said.

But still, I didn't fancy doing it. You see, I didn't want to annoy my gnomes. It would be horrible to shove them all into two big plastic bags. I might take them out next day and put them back on the shelves only to find that they were glowering at me.

Maybe they'd hate me to the end of time because I had once jumbled all of them up in two black plastic bags and left them out all night.

I really didn't want to risk it.

"No," I said. "We can't do that. We'll have to think of something else."

Alice and I sat on the back step and thought.

"How about buying another pack of bin liners?" Alice said. "Then they'd all have enough room to be comfy."

"Good idea," I said. "Have you got any money?"

"No," she said sadly. "None. What about you?"

"No," I said, like a sad echo. "None."

"Perhaps you could borrow some off Mum."

"If Mum had any spare money," I said to Alice, "she would have bought another pack of bin liner bags when she was last down at the shops. And she wouldn't have agreed to take all the old rubbish out of Mrs Fry's loft and spend a whole day trying to sell it at a car boot sale."

We sat and thought for a while longer as all my gnomes lay higgledy-piggledy on the lawn.

Then Alice shook her head. "They don't look *right*, do they, all in a tumble like that? Maybe we should put them into little groups, so at least they have somebody to talk to while you and I try to think what to do."

"You're mad," I told her. "You're totally *bats*."

But it gave me an idea.

Chapter 6
Party!

"We'll let them have a party," I told Alice.

"A *party?*"

"Yes. You thought they should all have someone to talk to while they're on the lawn. But we could make it even more fun for them. We could give them a party."

"A proper, grown-up, all-night party?"

"Yes. They'll love it."

Alice grinned. "*Much* more fun than sitting on a boring shelf in a boring garden shed."

"Or being stuffed inside a plastic bag."

"I bet they won't even mind if it's wet."

"I bet they'd *enjoy* it. Fresh rain on their faces. They'd think that was a treat!"

"And they are varnished," Alice said. But then her face fell. "What about the baby gnomes? They can't stay up all night!"

"There are only a few baby gnomes," I said.

"Still ..." Alice slid off the step. "I'd better sort out a babysitting place. Somewhere safe, where the little ones can be looked after and won't get into trouble."

I pointed. "You could use one of those old tyres off Nancy's van."

(Those tyres have been leaning against the fence for weeks now. First Mum thought she might paint them a nice colour and grow plants in them. And then she changed her mind. But no one has taken them to the dump, so they're just doing nothing.)

"Brilliant!" said Alice.

She went off to roll a tyre into place beside the shed, out of the wind.

Then she rushed up to her room to fetch the old cot blankets she uses to keep her soft toys cosy and warm. She brought down a few bath toys we keep because Alice still likes to muck about with them. And she brought down all the pretend food from her doll's house. Little wooden buns and sandwiches.

Then she came out with three plastic bananas. They were enormous – much bigger than the baby gnomes. But we didn't think they'd mind. "There'll be enough banana to go round," Alice said.

After that, she moved one or two flowerpots across, to make the area look pretty.

"There!" she said. "That's the nursery set up for the party."

"Awesome!" I told her. "Now we'll set up the grown-up party."

But no such luck. Just then, Mum called
from next door.

"Alice! Sam! I need your help."

Chapter 7
Ready to Rock!

Mum made us go up to Mrs Fry's loft and carry all the stuff that she was taking to the car boot sale down the stairs.

"Careful, dears! Mind my nice wall paper!" Mrs Fry called.

Then it all had to go out of the back door. ("Careful, dears! Don't let my paintwork get scratched!")

Then it all had to go out of her back gate.
("Careful, dears! Don't catch the lock!")

Then it all had to go along the alley to our
shed. (Silence.)

There was *tons* of stuff. Old fire-screens,
from when the houses had real fires. Rag rugs.
A set of wooden stools. Pictures. China plant
pots. Curtains. Lamps. Boxes of books. A few silk
dresses on some padded coat hangers. Three
different watering cans. Bits of old carpet.
(Alice bagged one, to make a dance floor for the
gnomes.)

I thought we'd never, ever, get to the end of carrying stuff. After we'd piled it all up outside the shed, Mum started to stack it in neat rows inside.

I was amazed it fitted in. But it did.

Just.

And then Mum let us go, so we went back to sorting out the gnomes.

I haven't been to many grown-up parties. But Nancy invites us round at New Year, and there are always lots of adults at her parties. I've also been picked two times to hand round the nibbles when parents come to school meetings. And I've seen hundreds of parties on films and telly.

I reckoned I could do it.

We unrolled the dance floor carpet, then set out upside-down flowerpots around its sides, to make the sort of silly little tables that people use for their drinks. Alice found three sheets of card, and cut them into gnome-sized circles for plates.

Then she made paper sandwiches.

I thought that was a bit silly. (Alice is only young.) I wanted them to have a much more grown-up evening, so I went looking for the box of chocolates Uncle Tom gave Mum at Christmas. All of the chocolates inside were in the shape of tiny bottles, and covered in shiny paper. They were all filled with different sorts of fancy alcohol. ('Liqueurs', Mum called them.)

Mum adores chocolate, but she doesn't drink. (She says she saw enough of that before Dad left.)

That's why the box was still there.

I put some of the bottles on the flowerpot tables, and others in neat rows along a table at the side (an upside-down box). I half blew up a few balloons left over from Alice's birthday. I strung some bunting Mum got for the Royal

Jubilee along the washing line, and Alice went off to sneak some clean sand from the play park down the street.

She poured the sand into tiny doll dishes and spread them round. (If you were gnome-sized, it would look a bit like peanuts.)

I wound up Alice's old wind-up toy radio.

And we were ready to rock!

Chapter 8
Grim! Just *Grim*!

It must have been a *brilliant* party. We didn't get to see it all. Mum sends poor Alice to bed at 8.30, and if my light's not out by 10, I'm in big trouble.

I fell asleep much earlier than that. (I was *shattered*. All that carrying!) But I sneaked a last peek out at 9.30, after I'd cleaned my teeth. The gnomes all seemed happy enough, sitting and standing in the same little groups Alice and I had put them in to get the party started.

By morning, it was a different matter.
When I woke up at 7.00 and looked outside, the garden was a mess.

Not just a little mess.

A big **mess**.

A huge, massive, giant, horrible, got-to-clear-up-before-the-neighbours-see-this **mess**.

Alice came charging into my room. She didn't even stop to knock. (She never does.)

"Sam! Have you looked? Have you *looked*?"

We stared out of the window together. The baby gnomes were tucked up safe and warm in the tyres, covered in cot blankets to keep them warm. But half of the grown-up gnomes were flat on their backs, and others had fallen under the flowerbeds. It looked as if several of them had bashed into one another, and fallen into an untidy pile on the dance floor. One of them was halfway up a bush, where he seemed to be stuck. Two looked as if they were fighting. Some others had been tied to their toadstools with bunting. And there had been a giant food fight because the peanuts – sorry, the *sand* – was sprinkled all over the lawn.

And there were bottles all over the place – not in neat rows, as I had left them the night before. Now they were lying all over the grass, as if the gnomes had swigged all the alcohol, then tossed the chocolate away without even looking for a bin.

"Look at the mess!" said Alice. "It's *disgusting*! They must have got so *drunk*!"

"Your paper sandwiches have gone down well," I said to cheer her up. "All of the plates are empty." (It was true – either the sandwiches had blown away in the night, or they'd been eaten.)

"I can't believe what I'm seeing!" said Alice. "They must have gone *wild*."

"That's drink for you," I said. "Mum's always saying so."

Alice shook her head. "It's a good thing the baby gnomes were all safe in their little nursery. But they must have been kept awake for hours with the noise. Most babies wake up early, but look, they're all still fast asleep." She turned to me. "Good thing their parents will be back in the shed tonight!"

"They wouldn't want another party tonight anyway," I told her. "Not a second night in a row. They all must feel awful this morning. Grim. Just *grim*."

"And very ashamed, I hope!" said Alice. "Look at the mess they've left us to clear up!"

Chapter 9
It's Money, Sam!

It didn't take too long to clear the lawn. The gnomes looked so beat up that I didn't think they'd mind the peace and quiet of a plastic bin bag. So Alice and I tidied them away into two of those, before we cleared up everything else.

I took what was left of the Jubilee bunting inside the house, to give it back to Mum. I found her sitting at the breakfast bar with Nancy. They were giggling.

"Do you want some help loading all that
stuff for the car boot sale?" I asked Nancy.

She laughed. "Sam, we did most of that
hours ago. Before you two even woke up. There
are just one or two more things in the shed to
take. But most of it's already in the van ready
to go."

"Except for you," said Mum. "So run up
and fetch Alice. Tell her to hurry up and get
dressed. And you. You're coming as well."

"Me? Why me? Why can't I stay home by myself?"

"Because you *can't*."

I could tell Mum wasn't in the mood to argue, so I went up to get Alice. Then I got dressed. By the time we had gobbled down our toast, Nancy was waiting in the van, and Mum was tapping her foot by the door.

"Hurry up, both of you!"

We hurried up. The drive only took twenty minutes. We found our official spot, and we unpacked the van. Nancy and Mum spread out Mrs Fry's old things, trying to make it all look a bit like an antique shop. They unrolled the rugs, and hung the dresses on the back of the van, and put the china pots round the edge.

I carried over the last two black plastic bags I'd found in the back of the van.

"What's in those?" Mum asked. "I was sure we had everything set out already."

"Well, these two bags were in the van," I said, and looked inside them.

My gnomes. Dozens of them. All tumbled together.

"Oh, I picked those up," said Nancy. "I saw the two bags lying outside the shed, and I thought you meant to bring them along."

"They're not for sale!" I insisted.

"But you can spread them round," said Mum. "It might help. They're such a creepy-looking bunch. People might stop to look at them, and then decide they want to buy a lamp or a watering can. And the fresh air will do your gnomes a power of good, after that party."

Then she and Nancy fell to giggling again. What was *wrong* with them? They seemed so pleased with themselves. Anyone would think they'd done something really clever.

In the end, Alice and I ignored the two of them. We set the gnomes out in a ring around the fire-screens and stools and books and pictures.

And then we sat and waited.

We didn't have to wait for long. The early bird bargain-hunters were there one minute after nine.

"How much is that gnome?" one man asked. He pointed to one of the sad ones.

"It's not for sale," I told him. "It's only trying to clear its head, after a party."

The man gave me a very odd look. But then Alice started to argue. Not with him, though. With *me*! "Oh, come on, Sam! You have hundreds of gnomes. That's not even one of your best. Why don't you let this kind man buy it?"

"How much is it?" he asked again.

I didn't get the chance to answer. Alice piped up. "Only £2!"

"£2?" The man smiled. "A bargain!" He put his hand in his pocket and Alice reached out to take the money. As the man stepped away with my gnome, a lady who had been standing behind him stepped forward in his place.

"Can I have one too?"

She pointed to one of the grumpy old gnomes sitting on a log. "Can I have that one?"

"No," I began to say.

"*Yes*," Alice interrupted. "You can have any one you want." She turned to me and whispered fiercely. "Sam! It's *money*. And we haven't got any! And you can always make more gnomes."

"All right," I said. "Since it's *money*. But we mustn't sell too many."

Well, ho, ho, ho! It was a busy day. The gnomes went like hot cakes. By the time Nancy and Mum got fed up and packed the fire-screen and the only two china pots they hadn't sold back in the van, we only had four left.

Only four! Out of *hundreds*!

"I'm giving you five more minutes," Mum warned us. "Then we're off home."

Some people had been nice. Some had been very rude indeed. But the last people to buy gnomes were the rudest of all. "Hey, Linda!" the man called. "Choose this one. This is the ugliest! It's *horrible*! Choose this!"

"No," his wife said. "This is the wobbliest. I want this wobbly one. I love the way it keeps on falling over."

"No – get this one. It looks so *stupid*! Its arms are dragging on the floor. Choose this one!"

I didn't care for their attitude. But Alice didn't mind. She just kept on selling. "Now don't forget that all our gnomes are waterproof and you can leave them out overnight."

"Well, I wouldn't have them in the house!" the woman scoffed. "Not anything this ugly! Not in the house!"

"Nobody said that you had to buy one at all," I muttered.

"Be quiet, Sam!" Alice hissed. "Have you any idea how much money we've made so far?"

She whispered the amount.

I was astonished. "No kidding?"

"No kidding! So you be quiet, and let me sell the last few."

I snatched up my very favourite. (I call him Clement.) "You can't have this one."

"All right," said Alice. "You can keep *one*. Just *one*."

And then, since the couple couldn't decide between ugly and wobbly and stupid, Alice sold them all three.

So I have Clement. I'm allowed to keep him on the shelf on the landing. (Mum says I can because there's only one of him.) Alice blows him a kiss each time she passes him. I simply nod hello.

I cannot wait to make more gnomes so we can make more money. I keep on seeing Mrs Pratt in the school corridor. "Can we do clay?" I keep begging her. "Please? Next art lesson? Can we do clay again?"

I watch her scurry away from me, and I don't mind too much. Even after Alice took her share, I still have lots of money.

And an empty shed (apart from two china pots and an old fire-screen).

I'm ready to start again.

Our books are tested
for children and young people by
children and young people.

Thanks to everyone who consulted on
a manuscript for their time and effort in
helping us to make our books better
for our readers.

More *4u2read* titles...

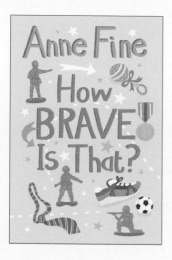

How Brave Is That?
ANNE FINE

Tom's a brave lad. All he's ever wanted to do is work hard at school, pass his exams, and join the army. He never gives up, even when terrible triplets turn life upside down at home.

But when disaster strikes on exam day Tom has to come up with a plan. Fast. And it will be the bravest thing he's ever done!

The Green Men of Gressingham
PHILIP ARDAGH

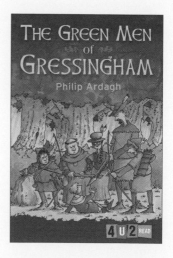

The Green Men are outlaws, living in a forest.

Now they have taken Tom prisoner! What do they want from him? Who is their secret leader, Robyn-in-the-Hat? And whose side should Tom be on?

Hostage
MALORIE BLACKMAN

"I'll make sure your dad never sees you again!"

Blindfolded. Alone. Angela has no idea where she is or what will happen next. The only thing she knows is she's been kidnapped. Is she brave enough to escape?

The Red Dragons of Gressingham
PHILIP ARDAGH

The Green Men used to be outlaws. They lived in the forest and did brave deeds.

Now the Green Men are inlaws. They live in the forest and do... not very much.

The Green men are bored. They need some fun. They need a quest...

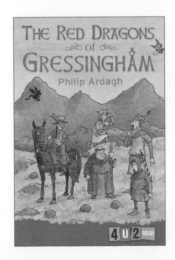

www.barringtonstoke.co.uk